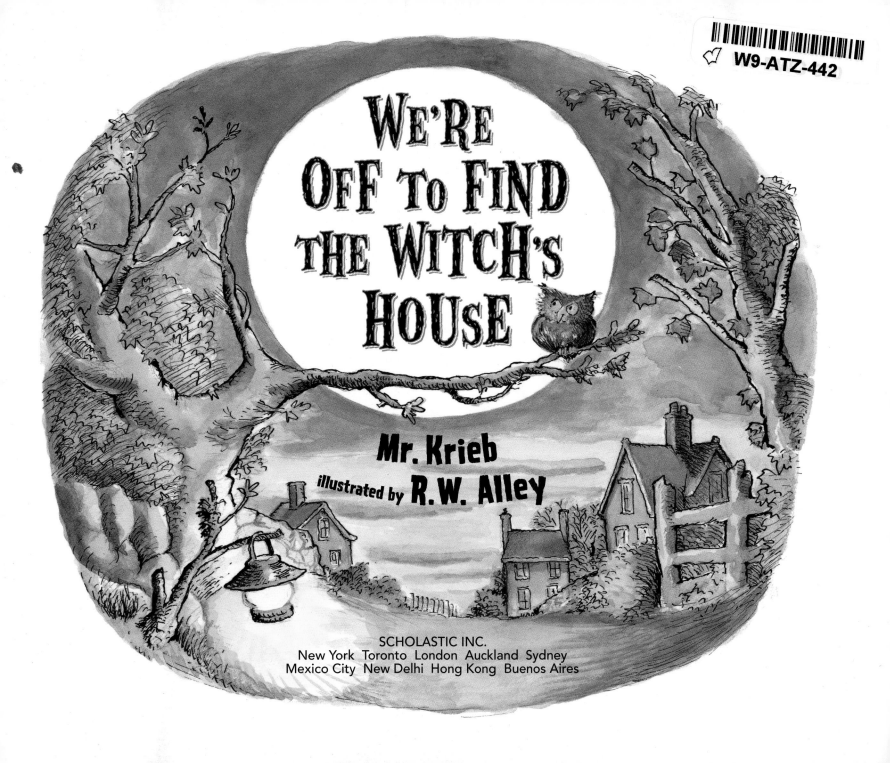

We're Off to Find the Witch's House

Mr. Krieb

illustrated by **R.W. Alley**

SCHOLASTIC INC.
New York Toronto London Auckland Sydney
Mexico City New Delhi Hong Kong Buenos Aires

ISBN-13: 978-0-545-10082-3
ISBN-10: 0-545-10082-8

Text copyright © 2005 by Mr. Krieb.
Illustrations copyright © 2005 by R.W. Alley.
All rights reserved. Published by Scholastic Inc., 557 Broadway, New York, NY 10012,
by arrangement with Dutton Children's Books, a division of Penguin Young Readers Group,
a member of Penguin Group (USA) Inc. SCHOLASTIC and associated logos are
trademarks and/or registered trademarks of Scholastic Inc.

12 11 10 9 8 7 6 5 4 3 2 1   8 9 10 11 12 13/0

Printed in the U.S.A.   08

First Scholastic printing, October 2008

Designed by Tim Hall

To all the delightful children with whom, for thirty years, I shared the tricks of imagination and the treats of language and laughter. Many now have children of their own who will soon be off to find the witch's house!
Mr. Krieb

For the tricksters and treaters of Hampden Meadows
R.W.A.

We're off to find the witch's house.

Which house?

The witch's house.

We're off to find the witch's house,
but we're not afraid.

No, we're not afraid.

We're creeping down the witch's street.

Which street? The witch's street.

We're creeping down the witch's street,
but we're not afraid.
No, we're not afraid.

We're slinking by a blinking owl, a winking owl, a blinking owl.

Wave good-bye to the winking owl, watching with one eye.

We're skedaddling past a skeleton,
a skittle-skattling skeleton,
a skinny, grinning skeleton, shake-rattling its bones.

We're bolting by big Frankenstein,
the herky-jerky, lurching kind—

his heavy head held on with twine.
Watch out! Don't get too close!

We're galloping past a ghastly ghost,
a mostly misty, ghostly ghost,

a flying, floating, twisty ghost,
swishing through the dark.

We're rambling past a howling wolf,
a scowling wolf, a growling wolf,

a hairy, scary, glaring wolf,
prowling in the park.

We're scrambling past Count Dracula,
a shirking, lurking Dracula,

with flowing cape spectacular
and fangs that glow so bright.

We're running by a mummy now.
I hope we'll make it by somehow.
I think I want my mommy now.
Here, hold my hand tight!

'Cause we're coming to the witch's house.
Which house?
The witch's house.
We're coming to the witch's house,
with bats and spiderwebs.

We're knocking on the witch's door.
Which door?
The witch's door.

We're knocking on the witch's door.

It opens with a . . .

SCREECH!

There she is—she's standing there!
She's standing where?
She's standing there!
There she is—she's standing there!

And we all scream . . .

Trick

Happy
Halloween!